▼▼ STONE ARCH BOOKS™

Published in 2014
A Capstone Imprint
1710 Roe Crest Drive
North Mankato, MN 56003
www.capstonepub.com

Originally published by DC Comics in the U.S. in
single magazine form as The Batman Strikes! #2.
Copyright © 2014 DC Comics. All Rights Reserved.

DC Comics
1700 Broadway, New York, NY 10019
A Warner Bros. Entertainment Company

Printed in China by Nordica.
1013/CA21301918
092013   007744NORD514

Cataloging-in-Publication Data is available at the
Library of Congress website:
ISBN: 978-1-4342-6484-8 (library binding)

Summary: The creature called Man-Bat escapes
Arkham Asylum with a secret weapon: a sonar
shriek that makes citizens turn "batty!" Can
Batman keep Gotham City from becoming a "City
of Bats?"

STONE ARCH BOOKS
Ashley C. Andersen Zantop Publisher
Michael Dahl Editorial Director
Sean Tulien Editor
Heather Kindseth Creative Director
Bob Lentz Designer
Kathy McColley Production Specialist

DC COMICS
Joan Hilty & Harvey Richards Original U.S. Editors
Jeff Matsuda & Dave McCaig Cover Artists

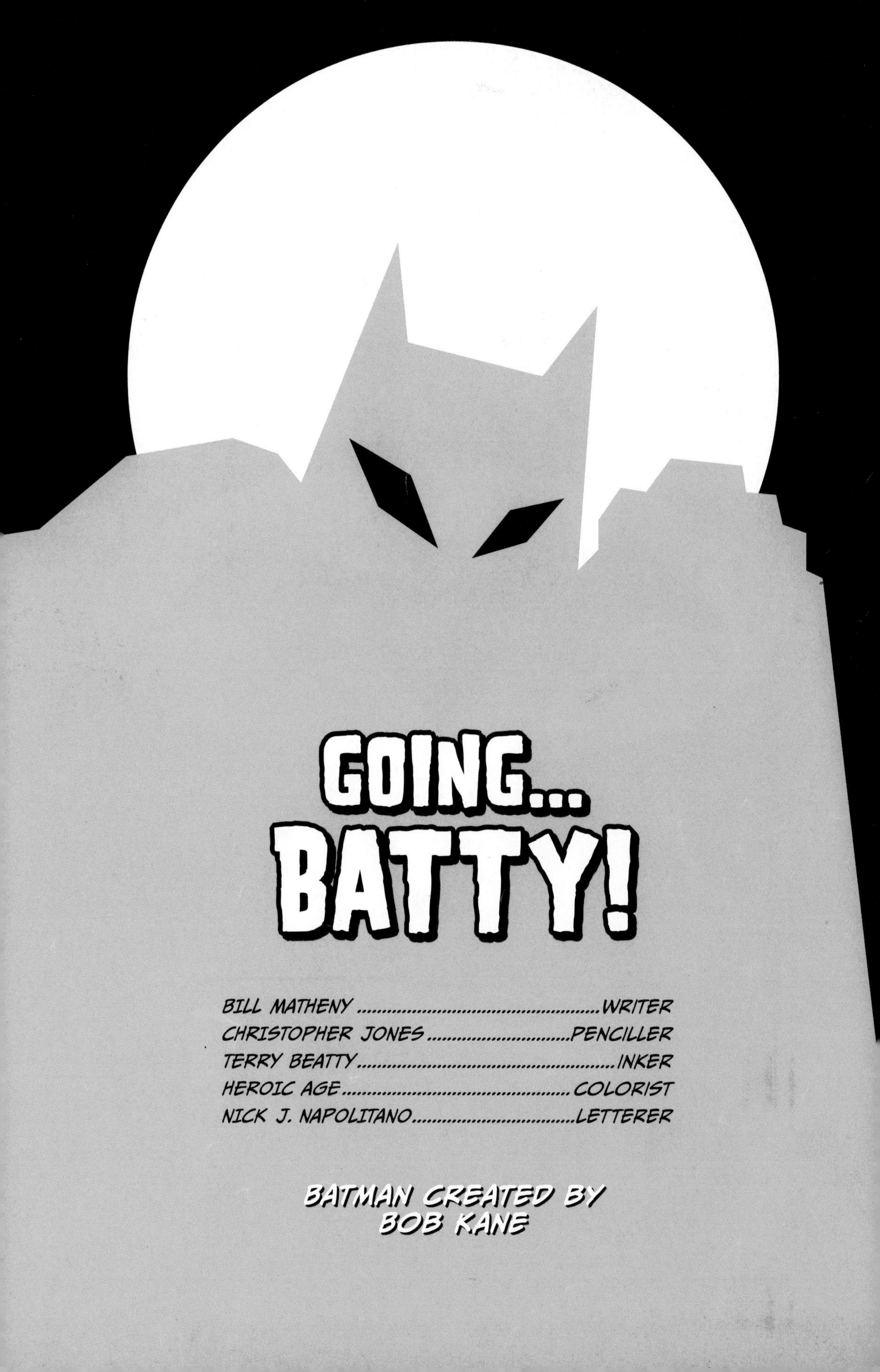

GOING... BATTY!

BILL MATHENY ....WRITER
CHRISTOPHER JONES ....PENCILLER
TERRY BEATTY ....INKER
HEROIC AGE ....COLORIST
NICK J. NAPOLITANO ....LETTERER

BATMAN CREATED BY
BOB KANE

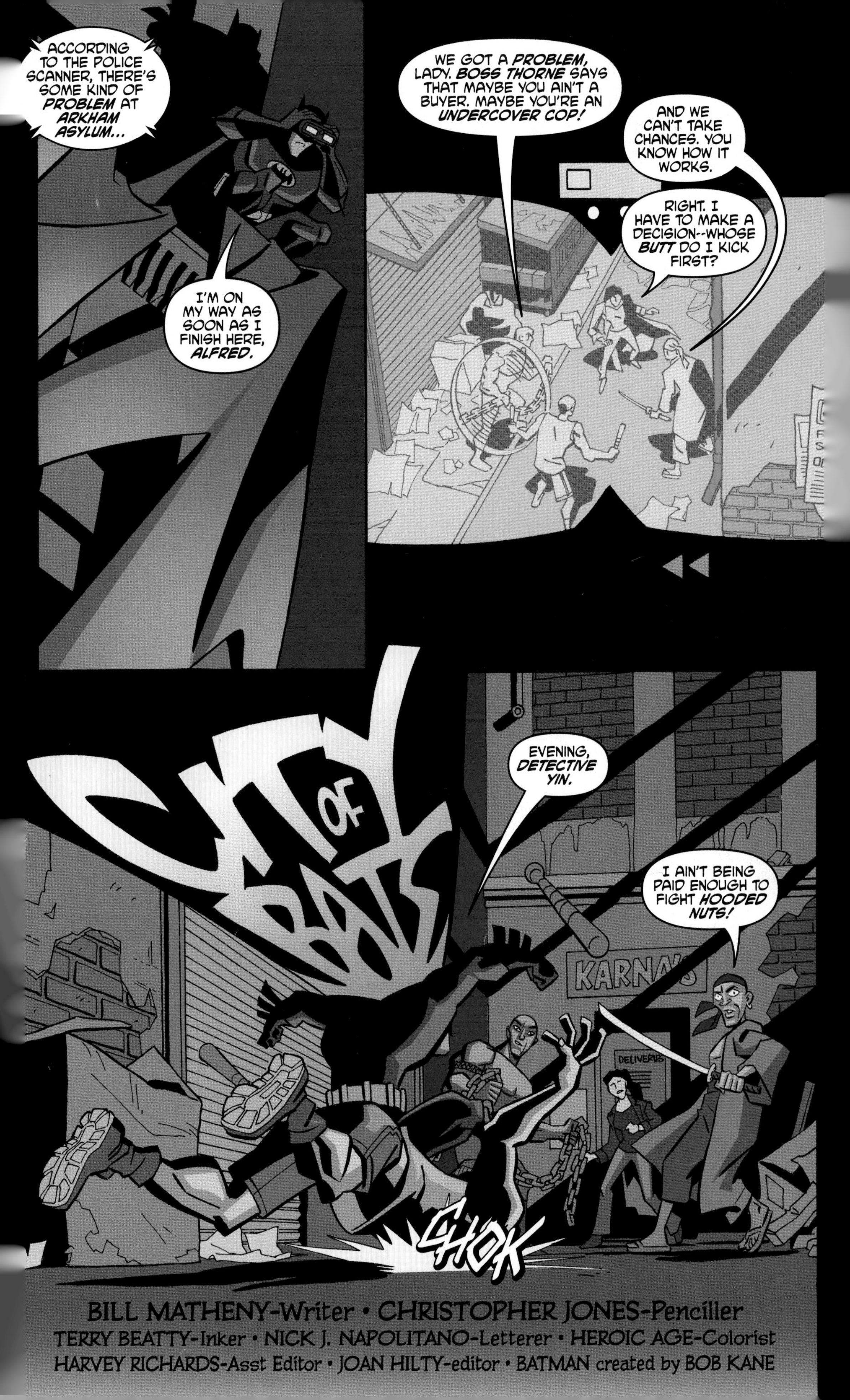

ACCORDING TO THE POLICE SCANNER, THERE'S SOME KIND OF *PROBLEM* AT *ARKHAM ASYLUM*...
I'M ON MY WAY AS SOON AS I FINISH HERE, *ALFRED.*
WE GOT A *PROBLEM,* LADY. *BOSS THORNE* SAYS THAT MAYBE YOU AIN'T A BUYER. MAYBE YOU'RE AN *UNDERCOVER COP!*
AND WE CAN'T TAKE CHANCES. YOU KNOW HOW IT WORKS.
RIGHT. I HAVE TO MAKE A DECISION--WHOSE *BUTT* DO I KICK FIRST?
CITY OF BATS
EVENING, *DETECTIVE YIN.*
I AIN'T BEING PAID ENOUGH TO FIGHT *HOODED NUTS!*
DELIVERIES
CHOK

BILL MATHENY-Writer • CHRISTOPHER JONES-Penciller
TERRY BEATTY-Inker • NICK J. NAPOLITANO-Letterer • HEROIC AGE-Colorist
HARVEY RICHARDS-Asst Editor • JOAN HILTY-editor • BATMAN created by BOB KANE

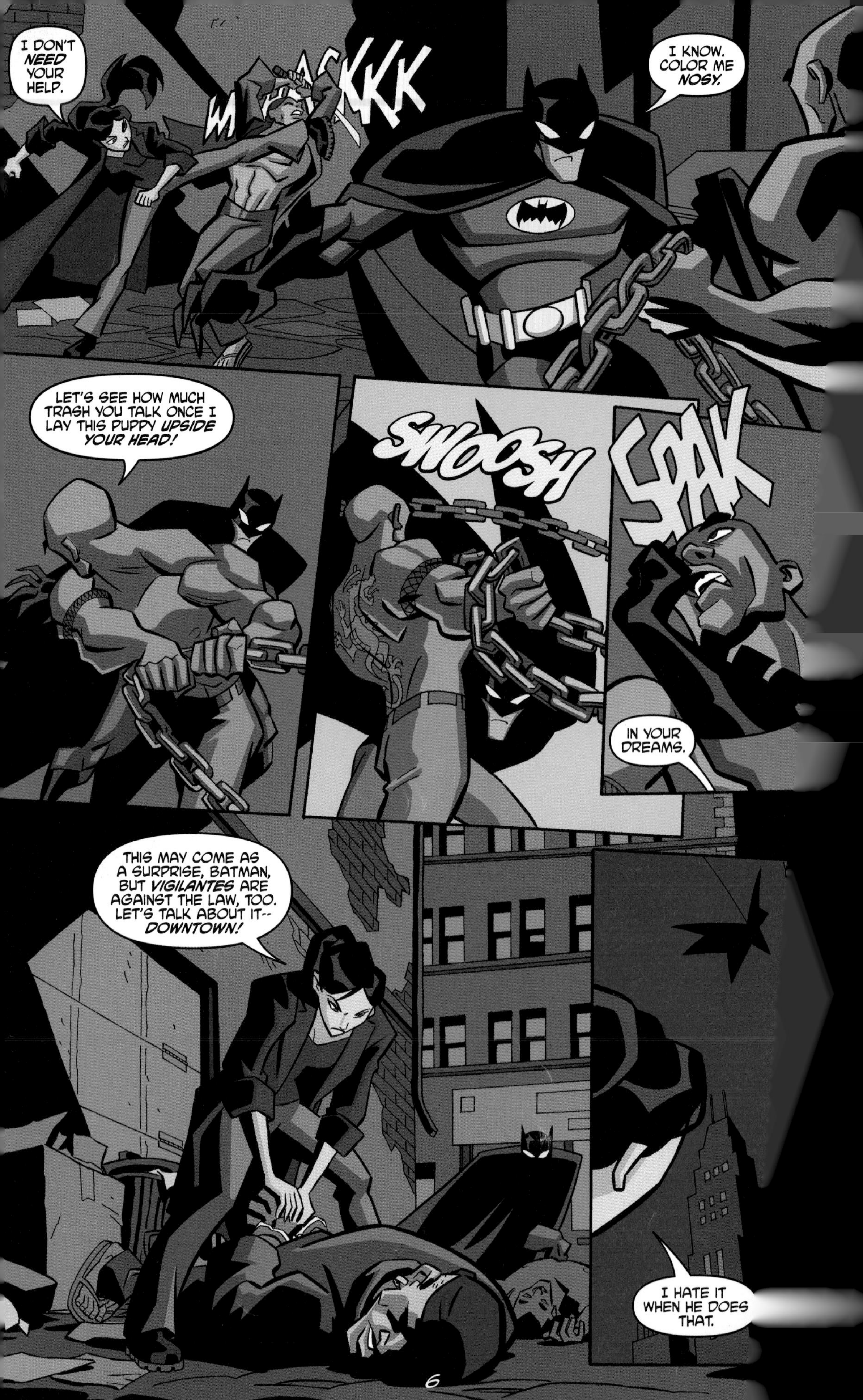
I DON'T NEED YOUR HELP.
I KNOW. COLOR ME NOSY.
LET'S SEE HOW MUCH TRASH YOU TALK ONCE I LAY THIS PUPPY UPSIDE YOUR HEAD!
SWOOSH
SPAK
IN YOUR DREAMS.
THIS MAY COME AS A SURPRISE, BATMAN, BUT VIGILANTES ARE AGAINST THE LAW, TOO. LET'S TALK ABOUT IT-- DOWNTOWN!
I HATE IT WHEN HE DOES THAT.

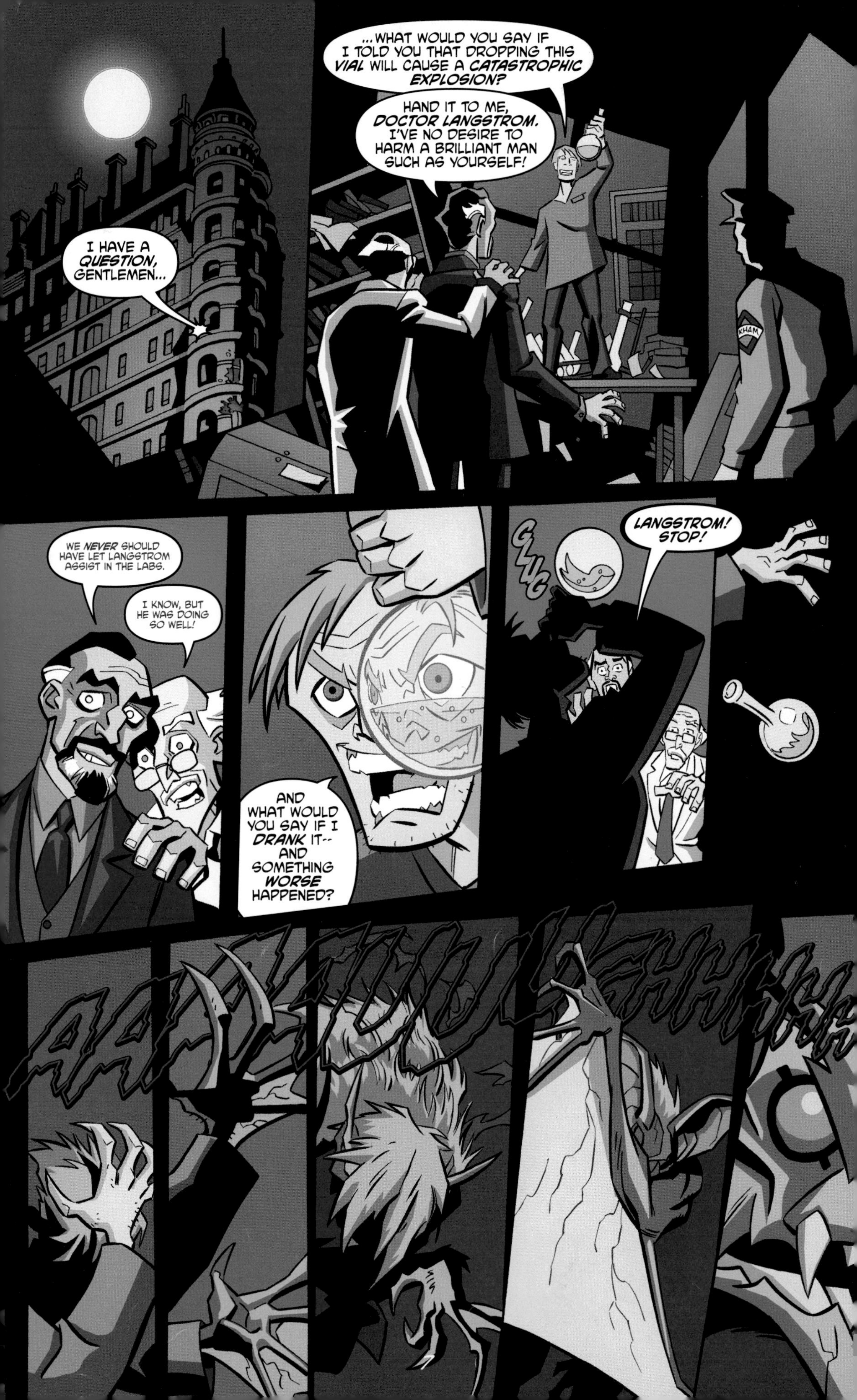
I HAVE A QUESTION, GENTLEMEN...
...WHAT WOULD YOU SAY IF I TOLD YOU THAT DROPPING THIS VIAL WILL CAUSE A CATASTROPHIC EXPLOSION?
HAND IT TO ME, DOCTOR LANGSTROM. I'VE NO DESIRE TO HARM A BRILLIANT MAN SUCH AS YOURSELF!
WE NEVER SHOULD HAVE LET LANGSTROM ASSIST IN THE LABS.
I KNOW, BUT HE WAS DOING SO WELL!
AND WHAT WOULD YOU SAY IF I DRANK IT-- AND SOMETHING WORSE HAPPENED?
GLUG
LANGSTROM! STOP!

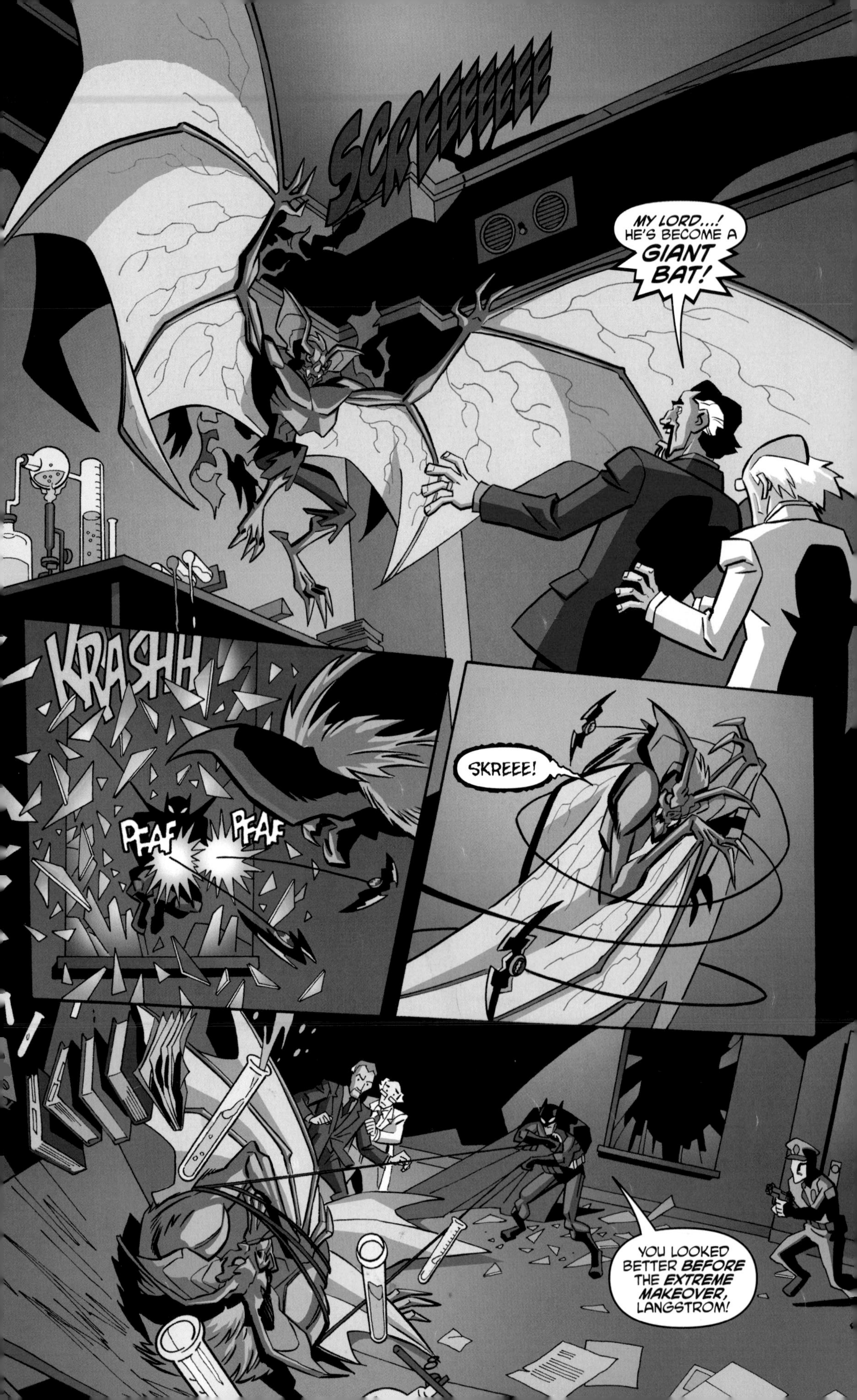
SCREEEEEEE
MY LORD...! HE'S BECOME A GIANT BAT!
KRASHH
PFAF
PFAF
SKREEE!
YOU LOOKED BETTER BEFORE THE EXTREME MAKEOVER, LANGSTROM!

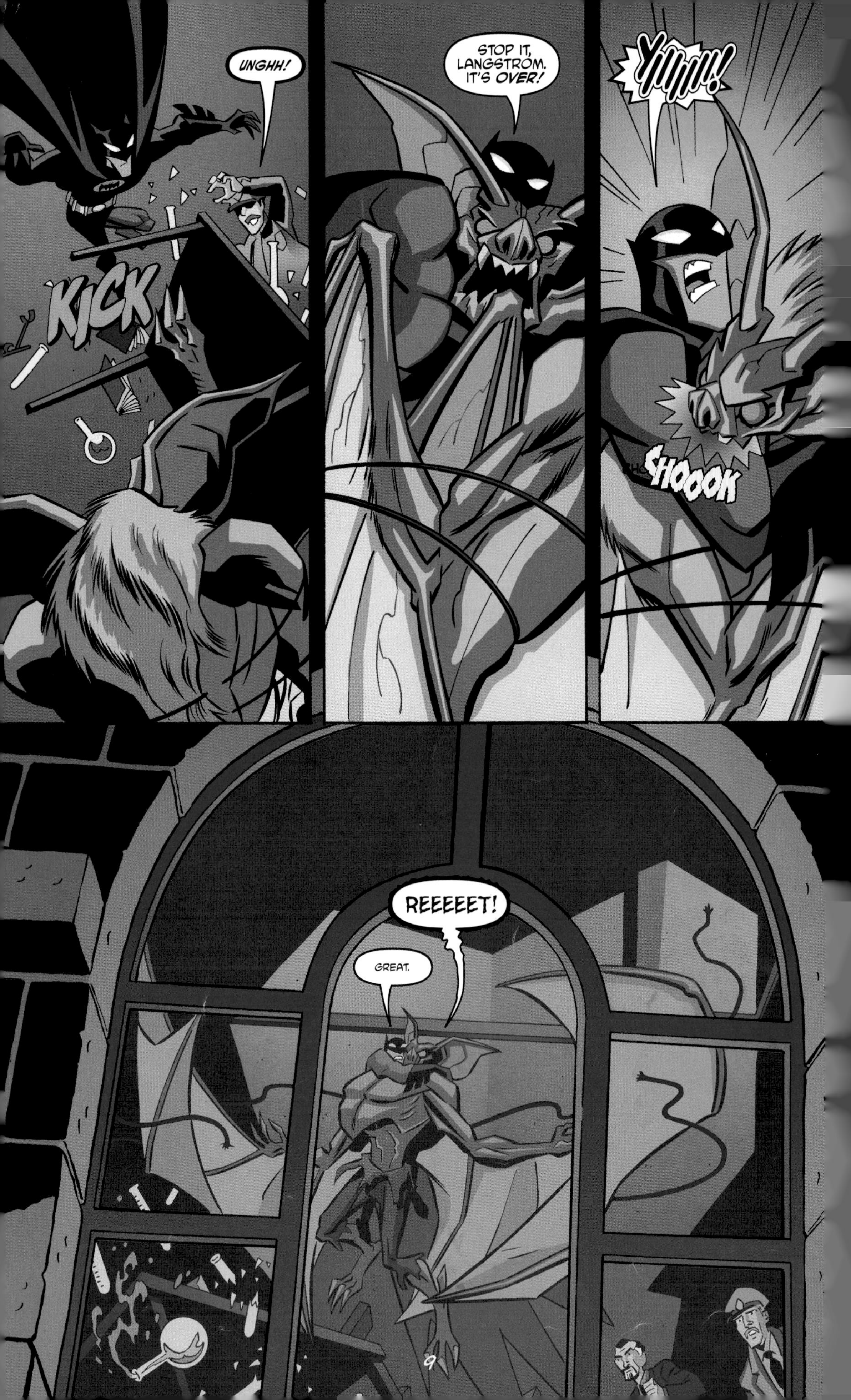

UNGHH!
KICK
STOP IT, LANGSTROM. IT'S OVER!
YNNNN!
CHOOOK
REEEEEET!
GREAT.

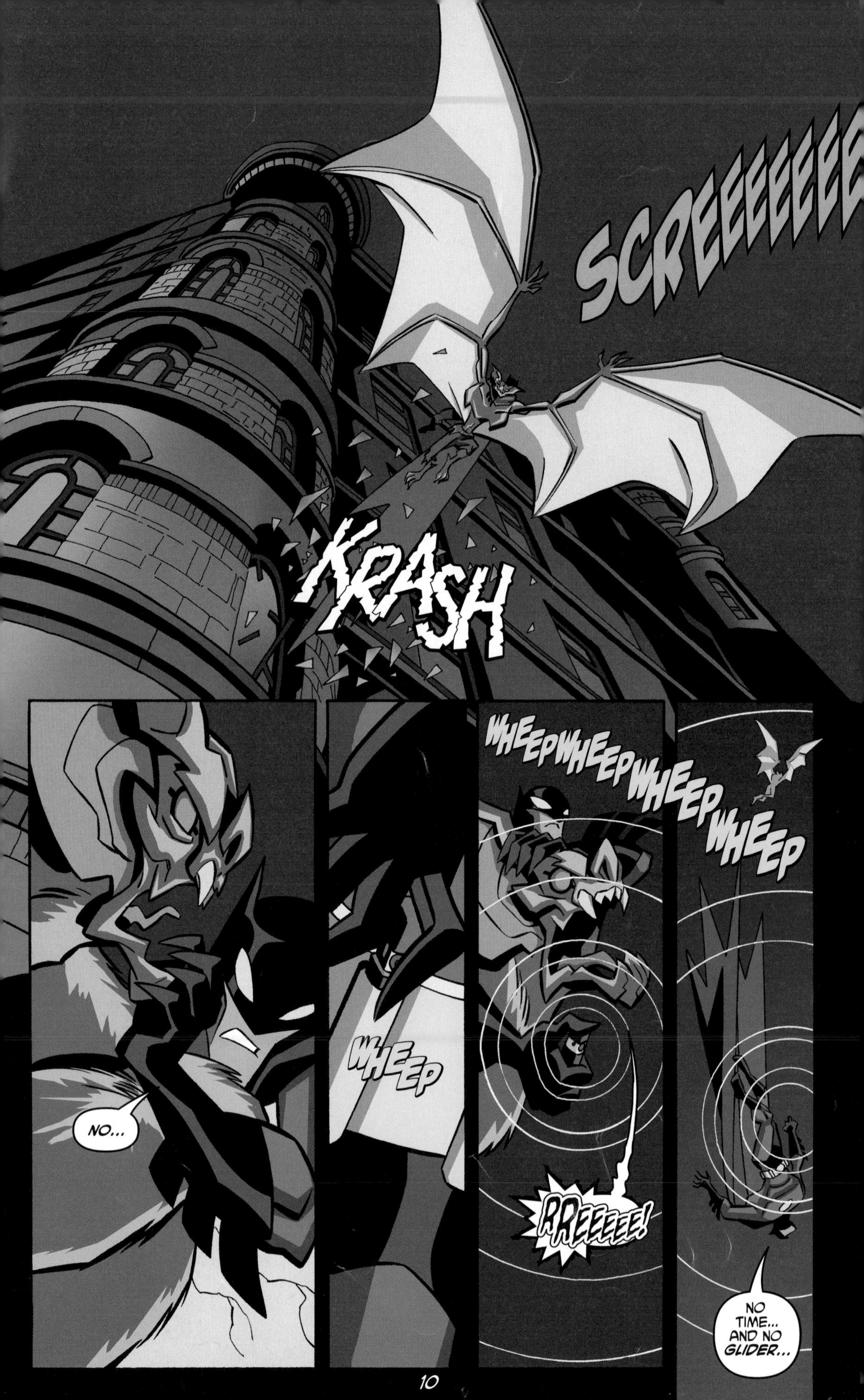

SCREEEEEEE
KRASH
NO...
WHEEP
WHEEPWHEEPWHEEPWHEEP
RREEEEEE!
NO TIME... AND NO GLIDER...

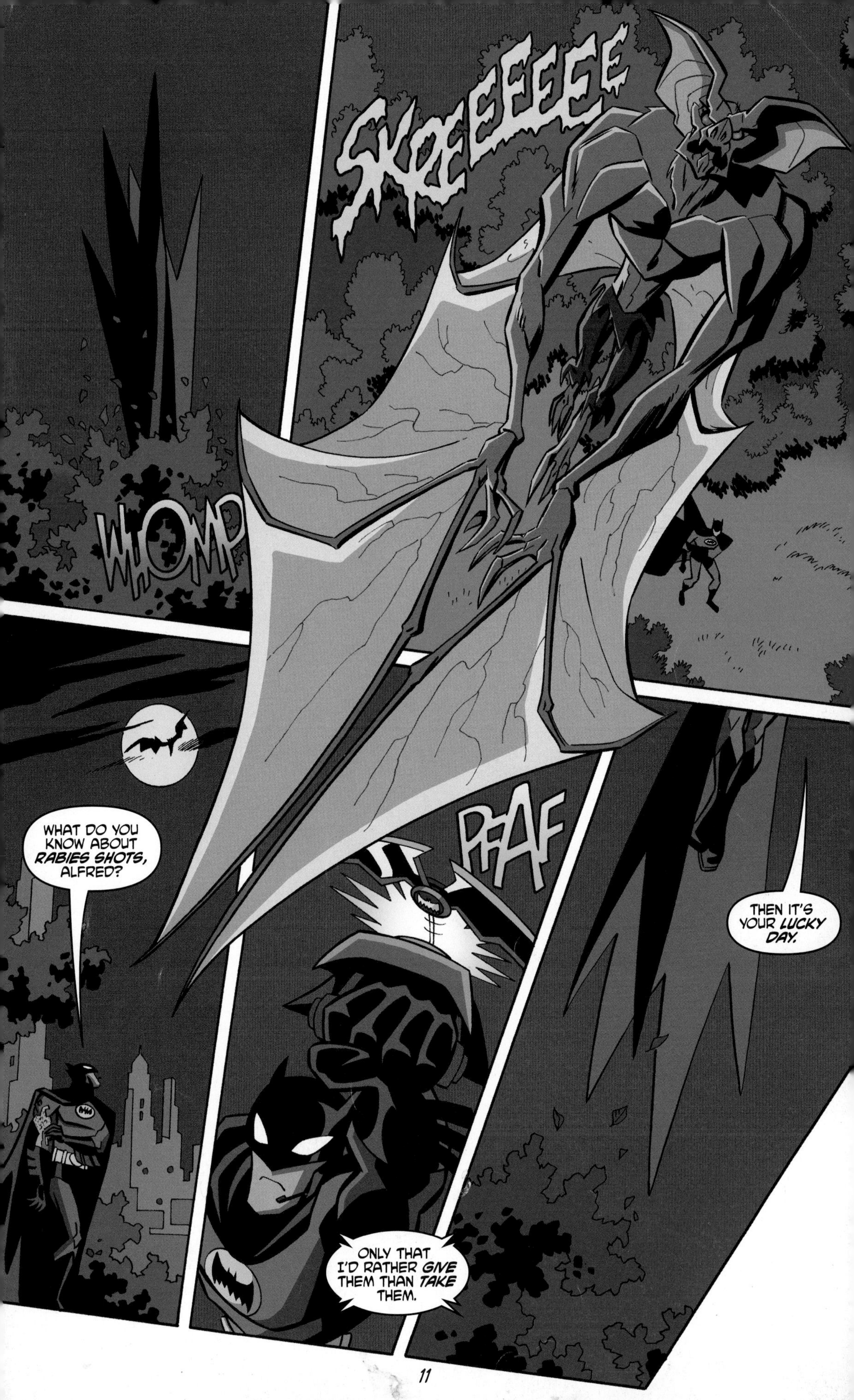
SKREEEEEE
WHOMP
WHAT DO YOU KNOW ABOUT RABIES SHOTS, ALFRED?
PFFAF
ONLY THAT I'D RATHER GIVE THEM THAN TAKE THEM.
THEN IT'S YOUR LUCKY DAY.

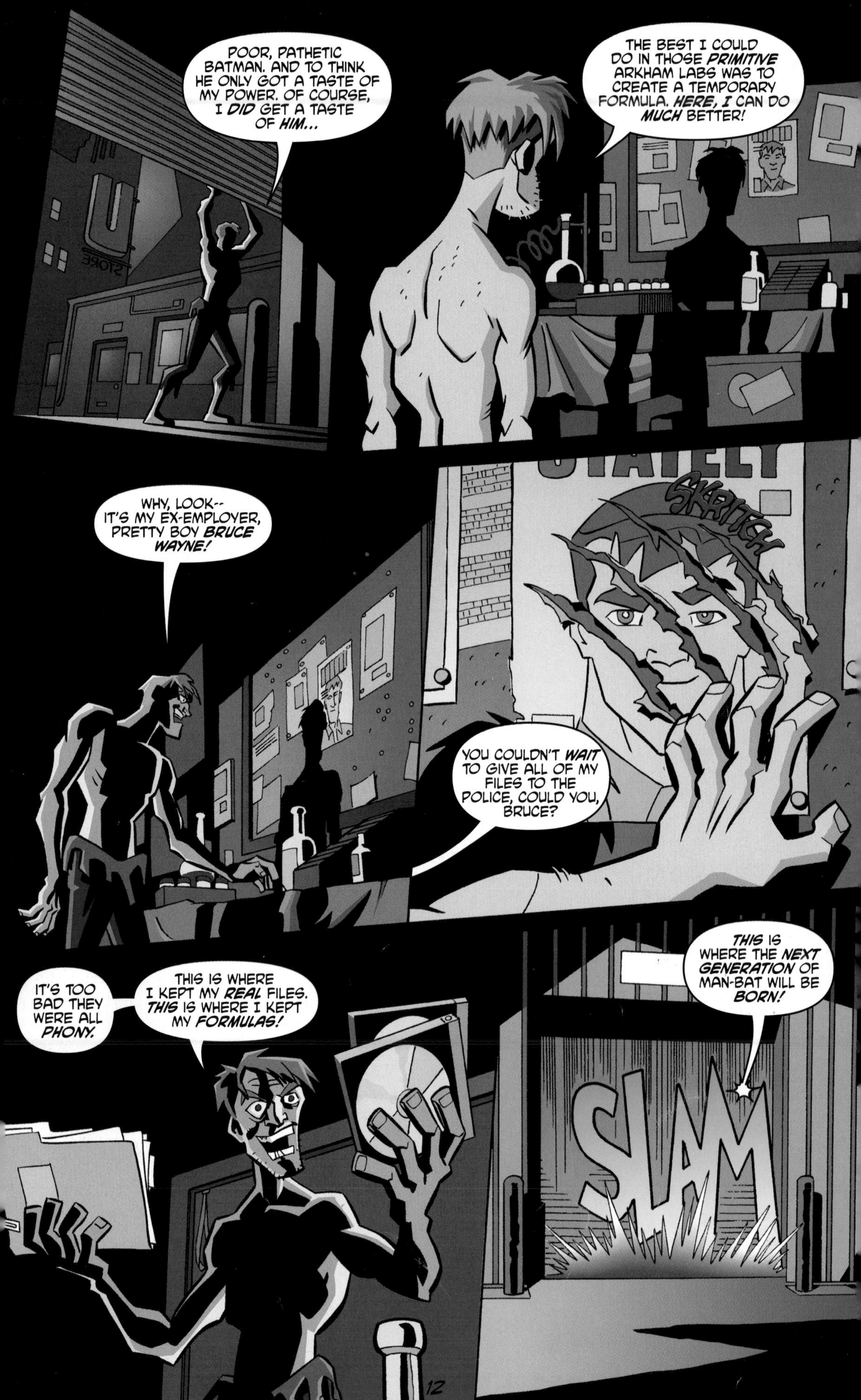
POOR, PATHETIC BATMAN. AND TO THINK HE ONLY GOT A TASTE OF MY POWER. OF COURSE, I *DID* GET A TASTE OF *HIM...*
THE BEST I COULD DO IN THOSE *PRIMITIVE* ARKHAM LABS WAS TO CREATE A TEMPORARY FORMULA. *HERE, I* CAN DO *MUCH* BETTER!
WHY, LOOK-- IT'S MY EX-EMPLOYER, PRETTY BOY *BRUCE WAYNE!*
SKRITCH
YOU COULDN'T *WAIT* TO GIVE ALL OF MY FILES TO THE POLICE, COULD YOU, BRUCE?
IT'S TOO BAD THEY WERE ALL *PHONY.*
THIS IS WHERE I KEPT MY *REAL* FILES. *THIS* IS WHERE I KEPT MY *FORMULAS!*
THIS IS WHERE THE *NEXT GENERATION* OF MAN-BAT WILL BE *BORN!*
SLAM

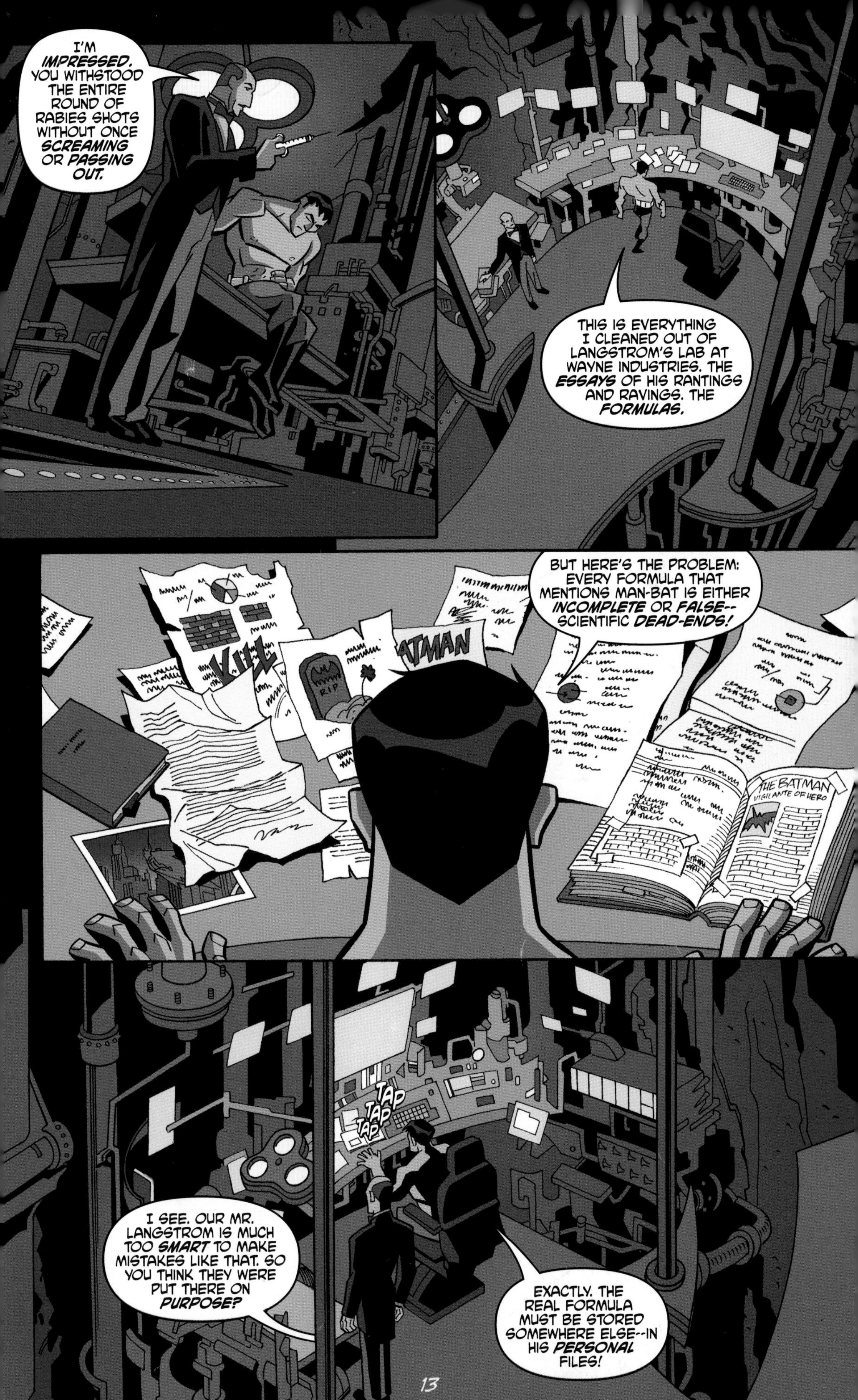

I'M IMPRESSED. YOU WITHSTOOD THE ENTIRE ROUND OF RABIES SHOTS WITHOUT ONCE SCREAMING OR PASSING OUT.
THIS IS EVERYTHING I CLEANED OUT OF LANGSTROM'S LAB AT WAYNE INDUSTRIES. THE ESSAYS OF HIS RANTINGS AND RAVINGS. THE FORMULAS.
BUT HERE'S THE PROBLEM: EVERY FORMULA THAT MENTIONS MAN-BAT IS EITHER INCOMPLETE OR FALSE-- SCIENTIFIC DEAD-ENDS!
KILL
ATMAN
RIP
THE BATMAN
VIGILANTE OR HERO
TAP
TAP
TAP
I SEE. OUR MR. LANGSTROM IS MUCH TOO SMART TO MAKE MISTAKES LIKE THAT. SO YOU THINK THEY WERE PUT THERE ON PURPOSE?
EXACTLY. THE REAL FORMULA MUST BE STORED SOMEWHERE ELSE--IN HIS PERSONAL FILES!

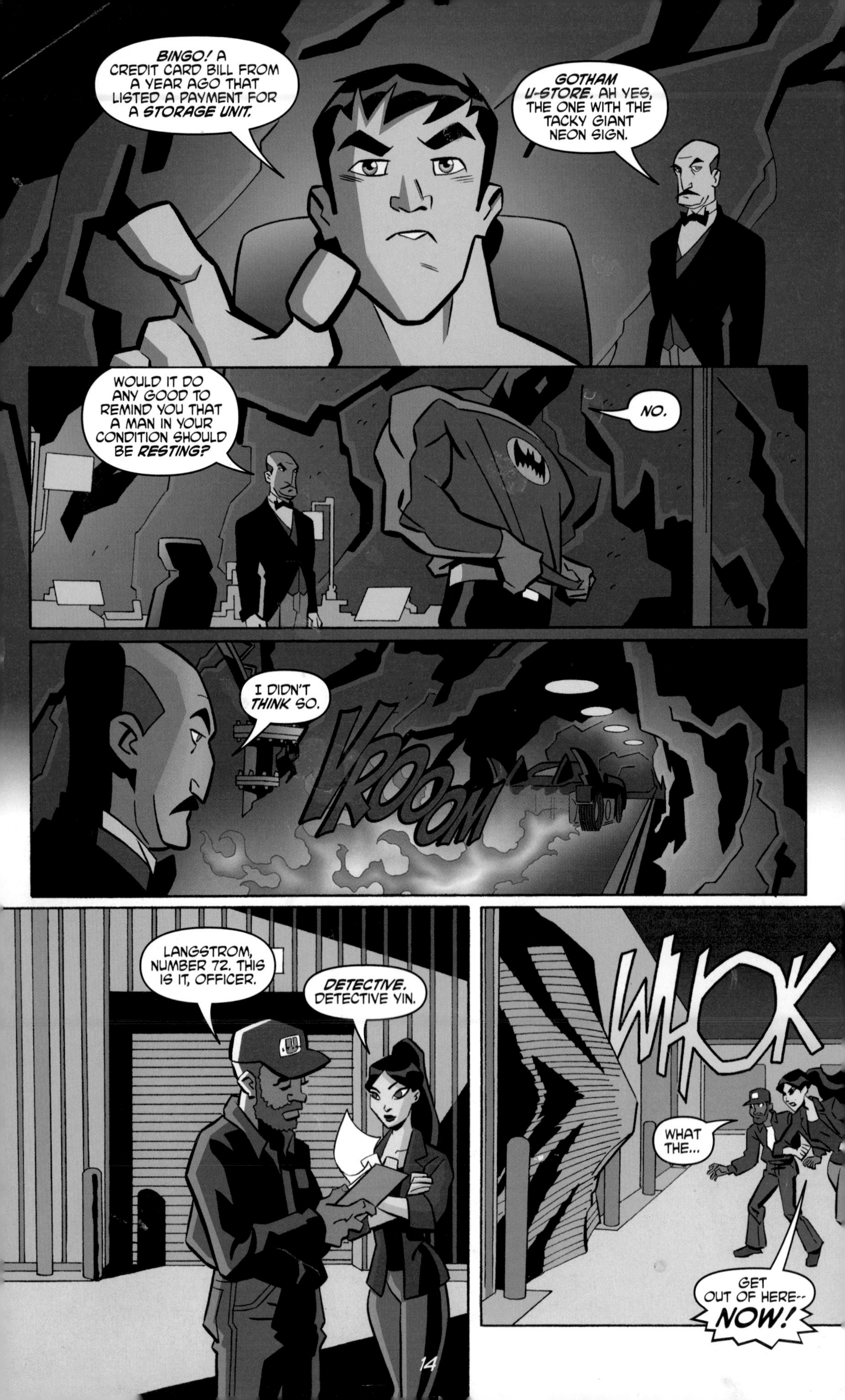
BINGO! A CREDIT CARD BILL FROM A YEAR AGO THAT LISTED A PAYMENT FOR A STORAGE UNIT.
GOTHAM U-STORE. AH YES, THE ONE WITH THE TACKY GIANT NEON SIGN.
WOULD IT DO ANY GOOD TO REMIND YOU THAT A MAN IN YOUR CONDITION SHOULD BE RESTING?
NO.
I DIDN'T THINK SO.
VROOOOM
LANGSTROM, NUMBER 72. THIS IS IT, OFFICER.
DETECTIVE. DETECTIVE YIN.
WHOK
WHAT THE...
GET OUT OF HERE-- NOW!

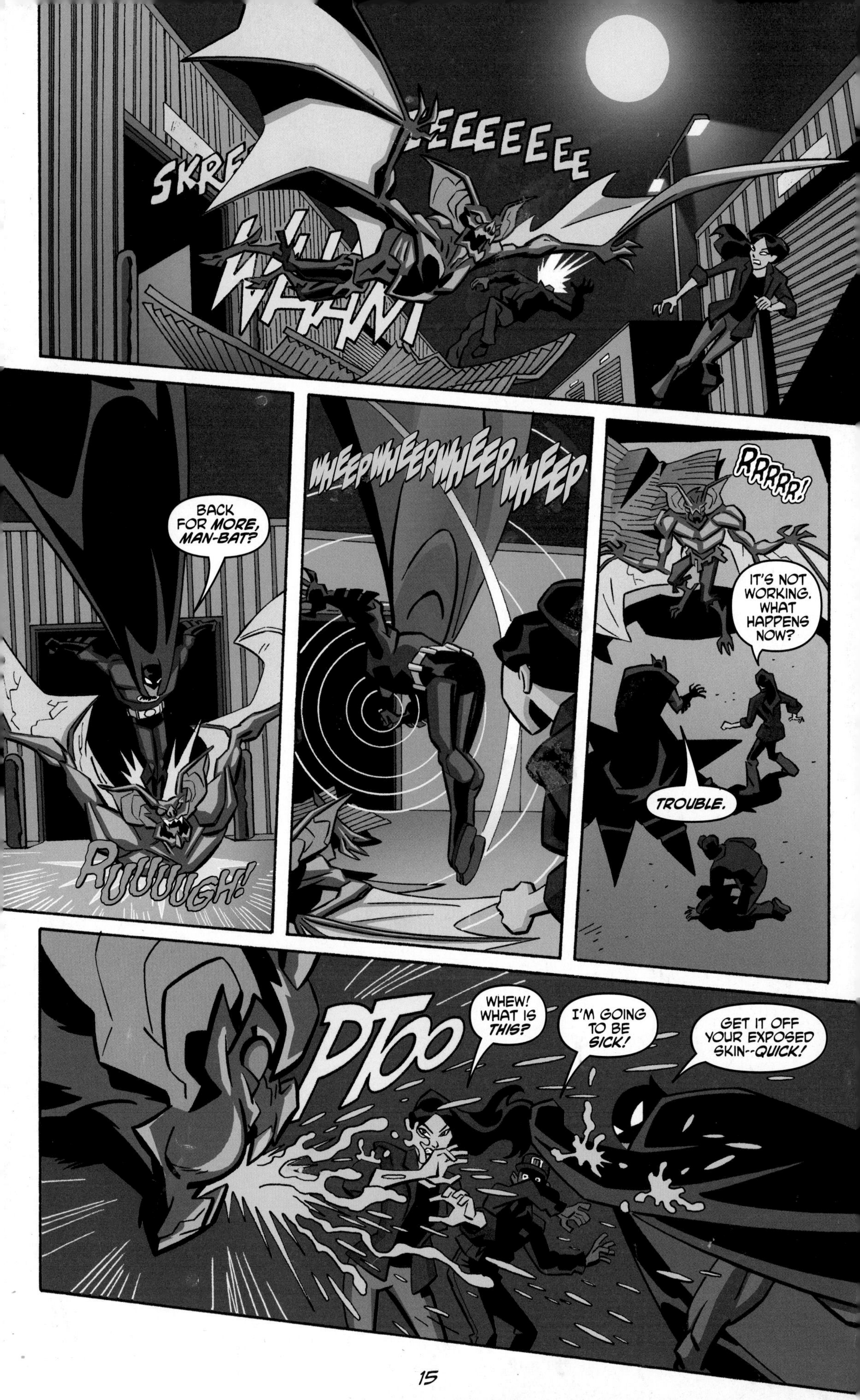
EEEEEEEE
WHAM
BACK FOR MORE, MAN-BAT?
RUUUUGH!
WHEEPWHEEPWHEEPWHEEP
RRRRR!
IT'S NOT WORKING. WHAT HAPPENS NOW?
TROUBLE.
PTOO
WHEW! WHAT IS THIS?
I'M GOING TO BE SICK!
GET IT OFF YOUR EXPOSED SKIN--QUICK!

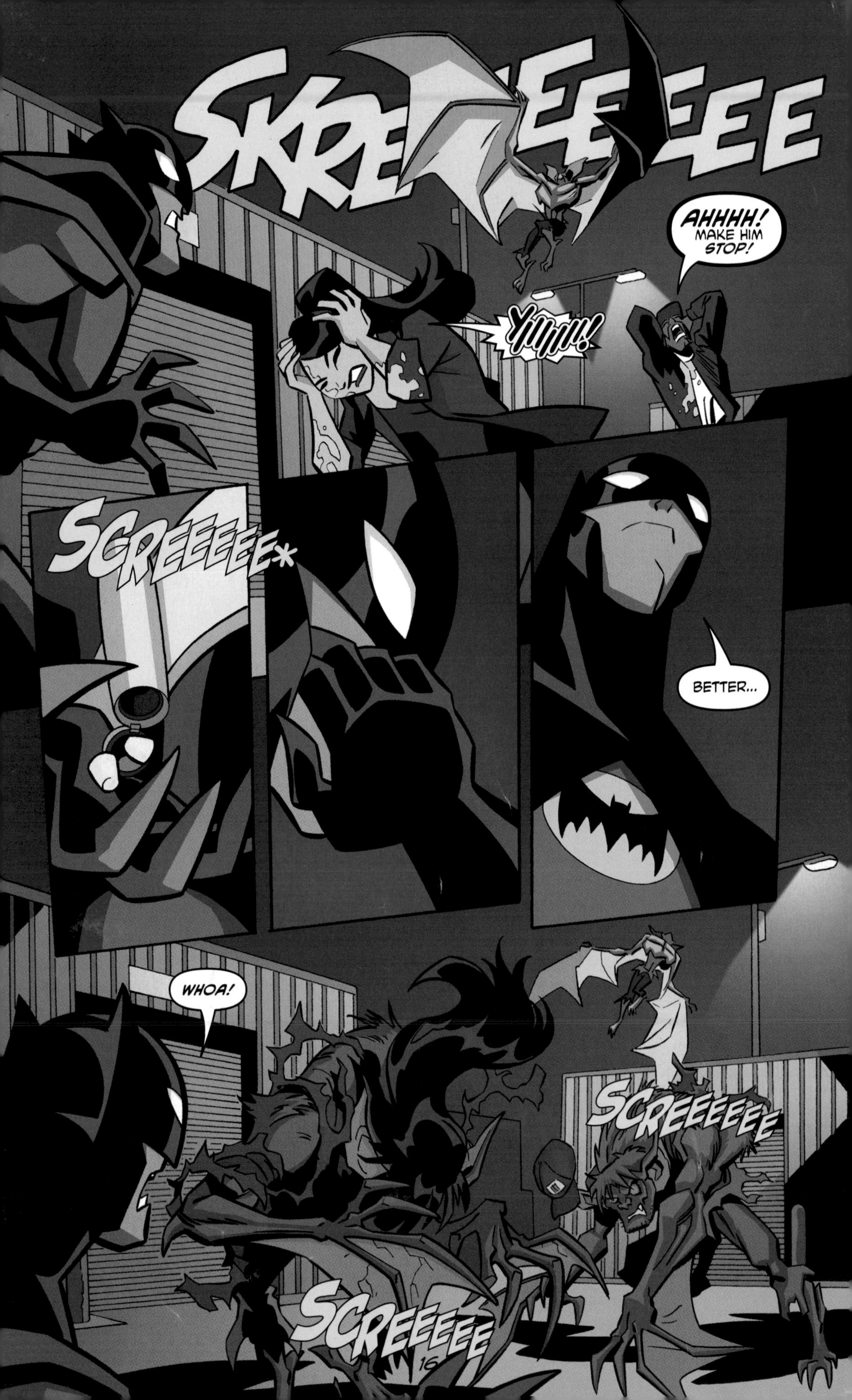

SKREEEEEEE
AHHHH! MAKE HIM STOP!
YAAAH!
SCREEEEEE*
BETTER...
WHOA!
SCREEEEEEE
SCREEEEEE

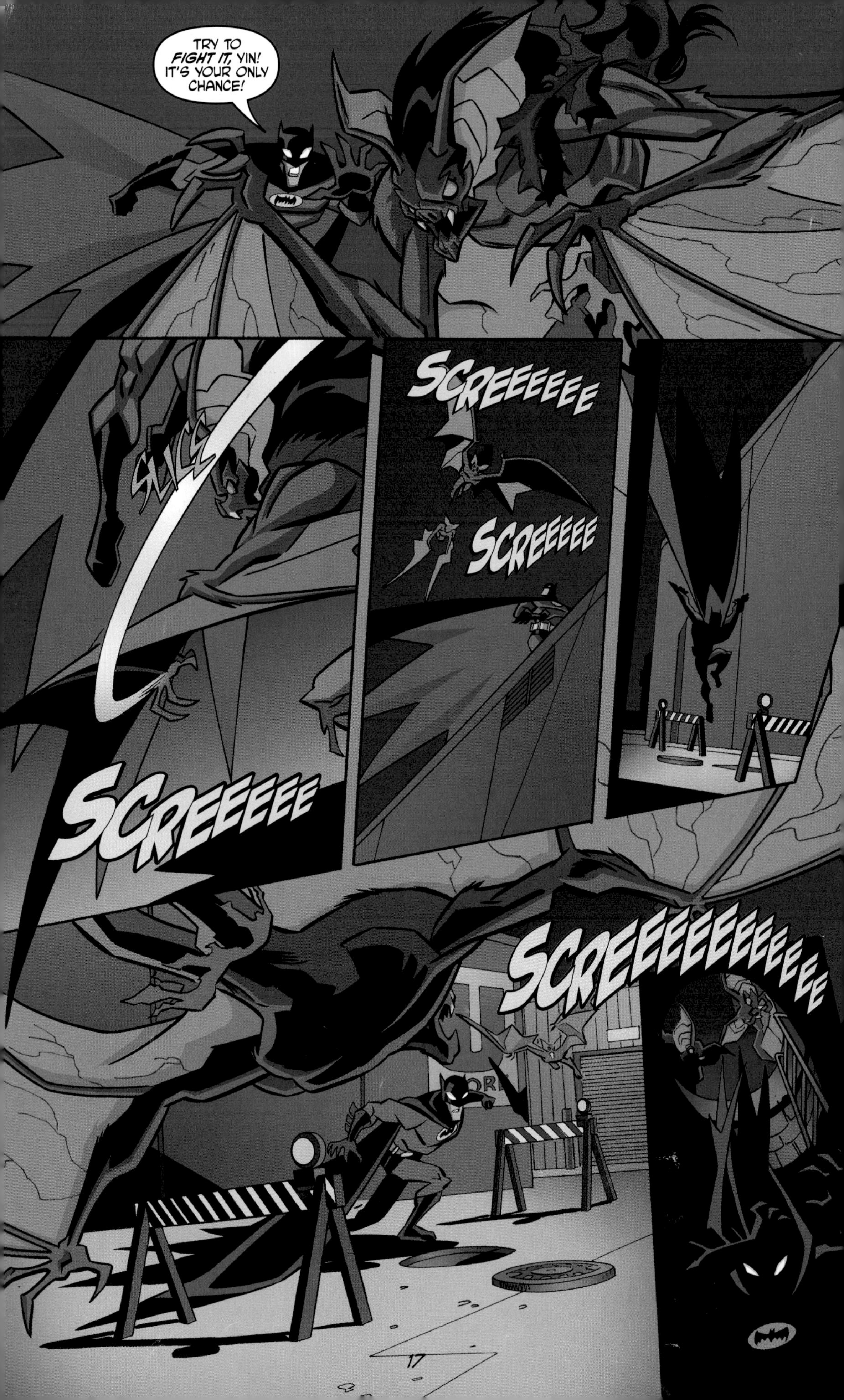
TRY TO *FIGHT IT,* YIN! IT'S YOUR ONLY CHANCE!
SLICE
SCREEEEE
SCREEEEEEE
SCREEEEE
SCREEEEEEEEEEEE

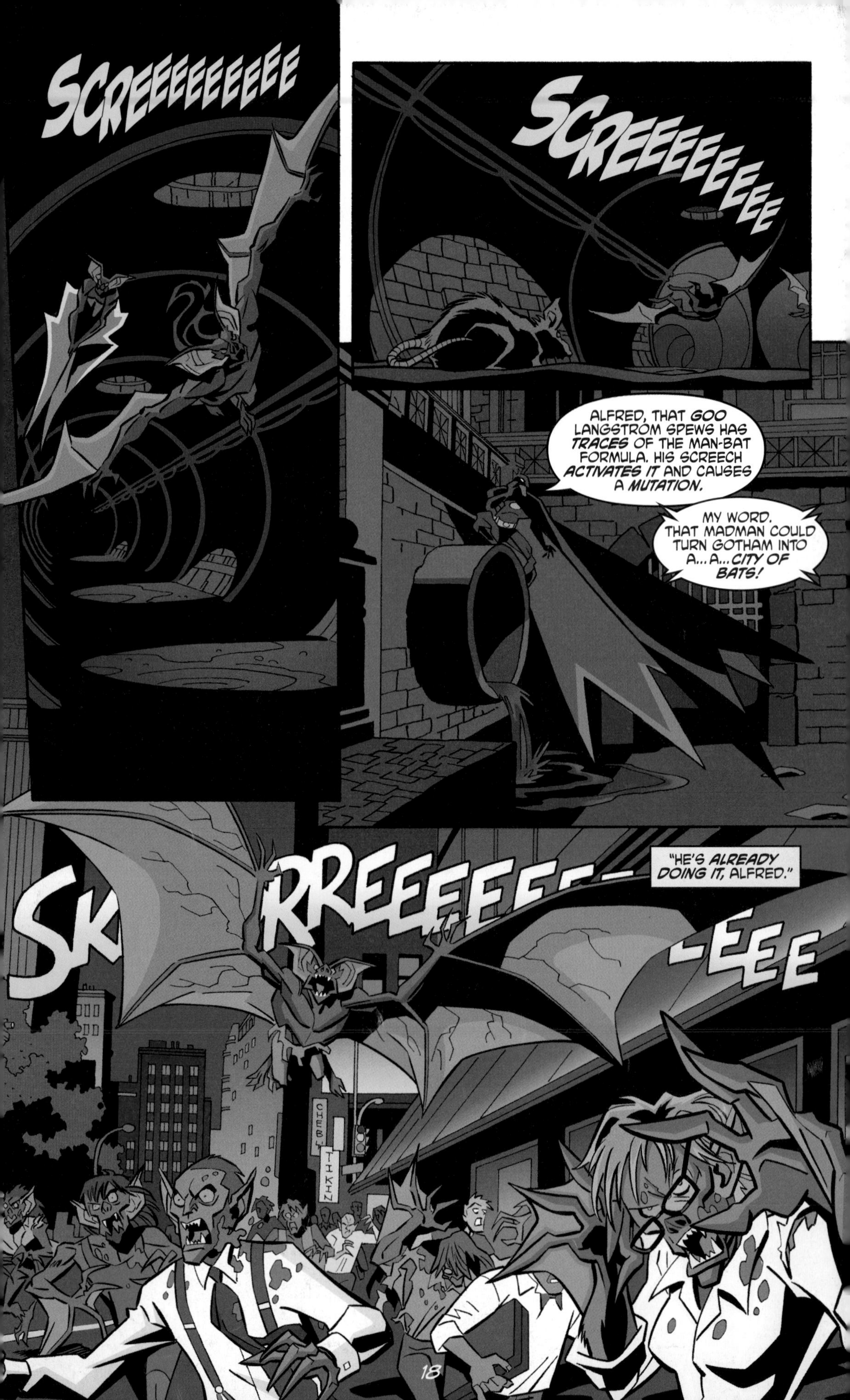
SCREEEEEEEEE
SCREEEEEEEEEE
ALFRED, THAT GOO LANGSTROM SPEWS HAS TRACES OF THE MAN-BAT FORMULA. HIS SCREECH ACTIVATES IT AND CAUSES A MUTATION.
MY WORD. THAT MADMAN COULD TURN GOTHAM INTO A... A... CITY OF BATS!
"HE'S ALREADY DOING IT, ALFRED."
SKRREEEEEE-EEEE
TIKIN

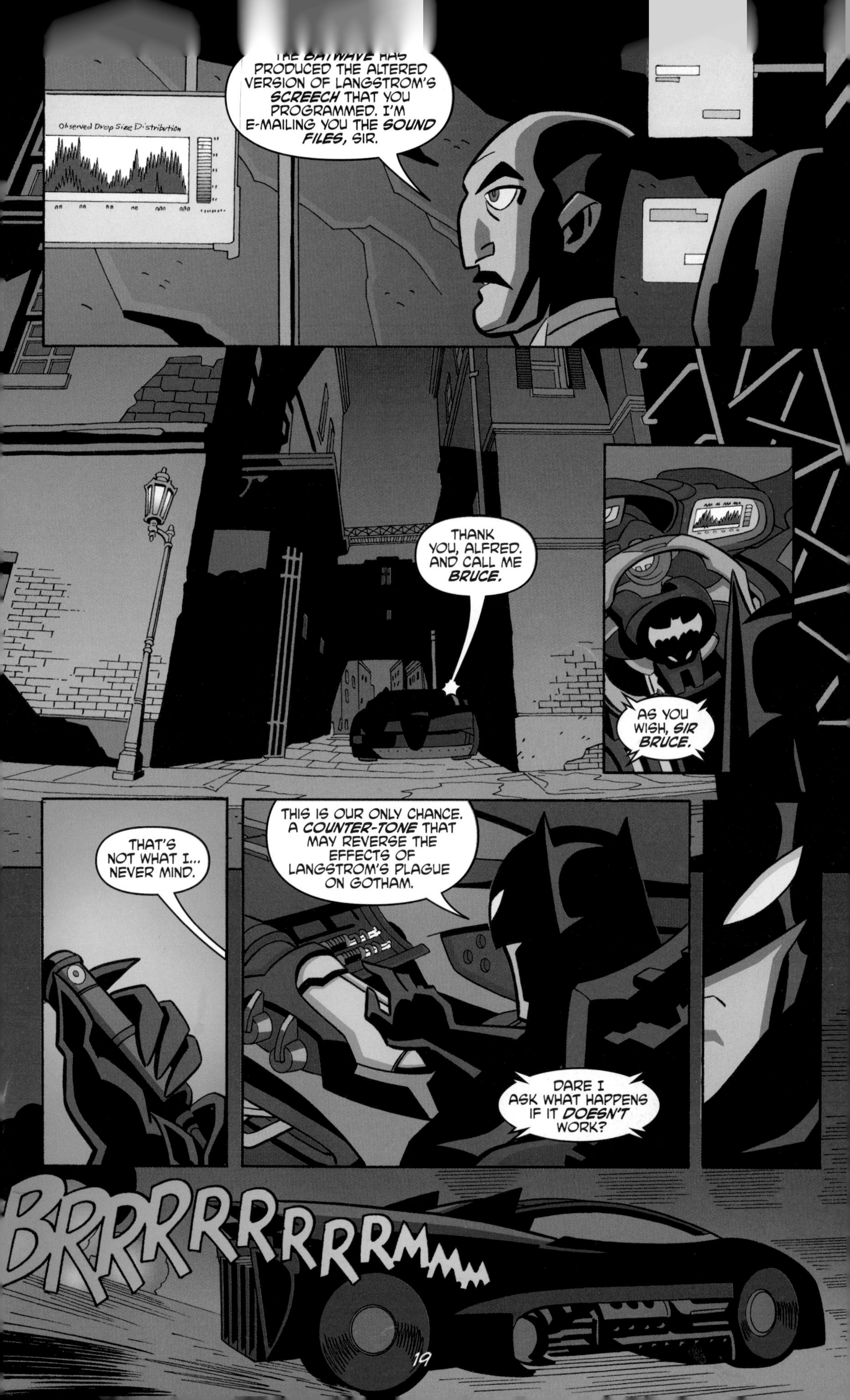
Observed Drop Size Distribution
THE BATWAVE HAS PRODUCED THE ALTERED VERSION OF LANGSTROM'S SCREECH THAT YOU PROGRAMMED. I'M E-MAILING YOU THE SOUND FILES, SIR.
THANK YOU, ALFRED. AND CALL ME BRUCE.
AS YOU WISH, SIR BRUCE.
THAT'S NOT WHAT I... NEVER MIND.
THIS IS OUR ONLY CHANCE. A COUNTER-TONE THAT MAY REVERSE THE EFFECTS OF LANGSTROM'S PLAGUE ON GOTHAM.
DARE I ASK WHAT HAPPENS IF IT DOESN'T WORK?
BRRRRRRRRMMMM

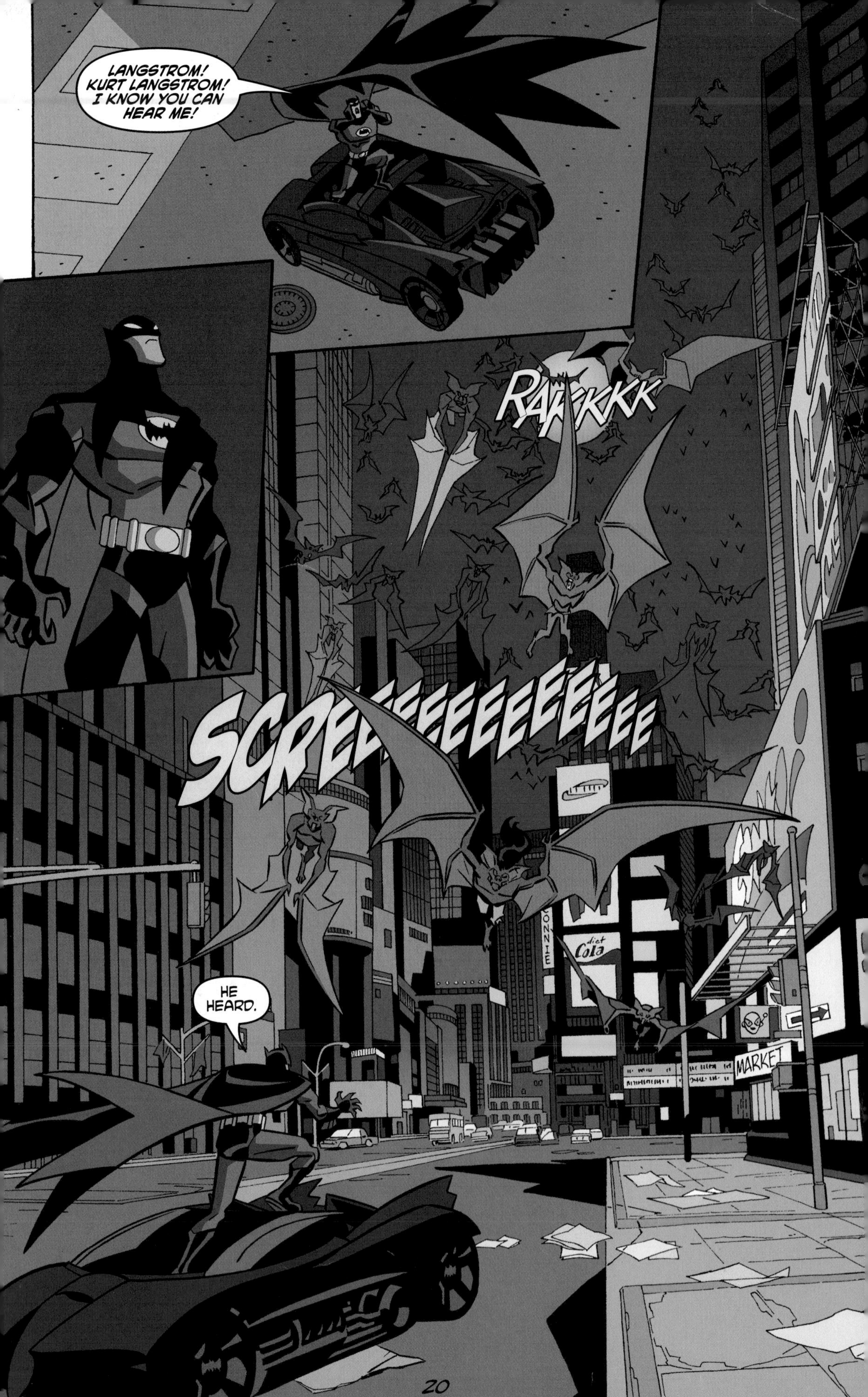

LANGSTROM! KURT LANGSTROM! I KNOW YOU CAN HEAR ME!
HE HEARD.
diet Cola
MARKET

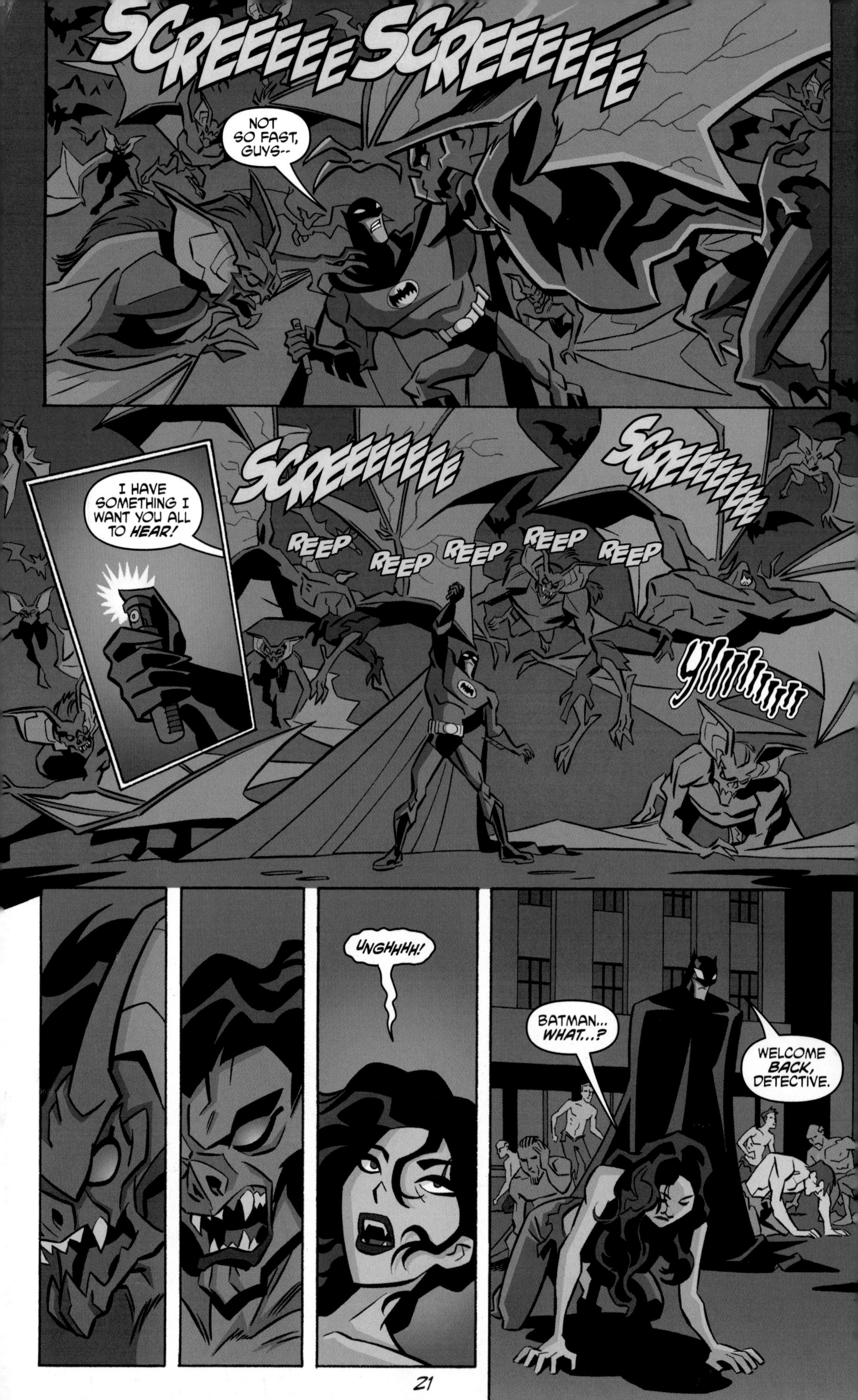
SCREEEEEE SCREEEEEEE
NOT SO FAST, GUYS--
SCREEEEEEEE
SCREEEEEEEE
I HAVE SOMETHING I WANT YOU ALL TO *HEAR!*
REEP
REEP
REEP
REEP
REEP
UNGHHHH!
BATMAN... *WHAT...?*
WELCOME *BACK,* DETECTIVE.

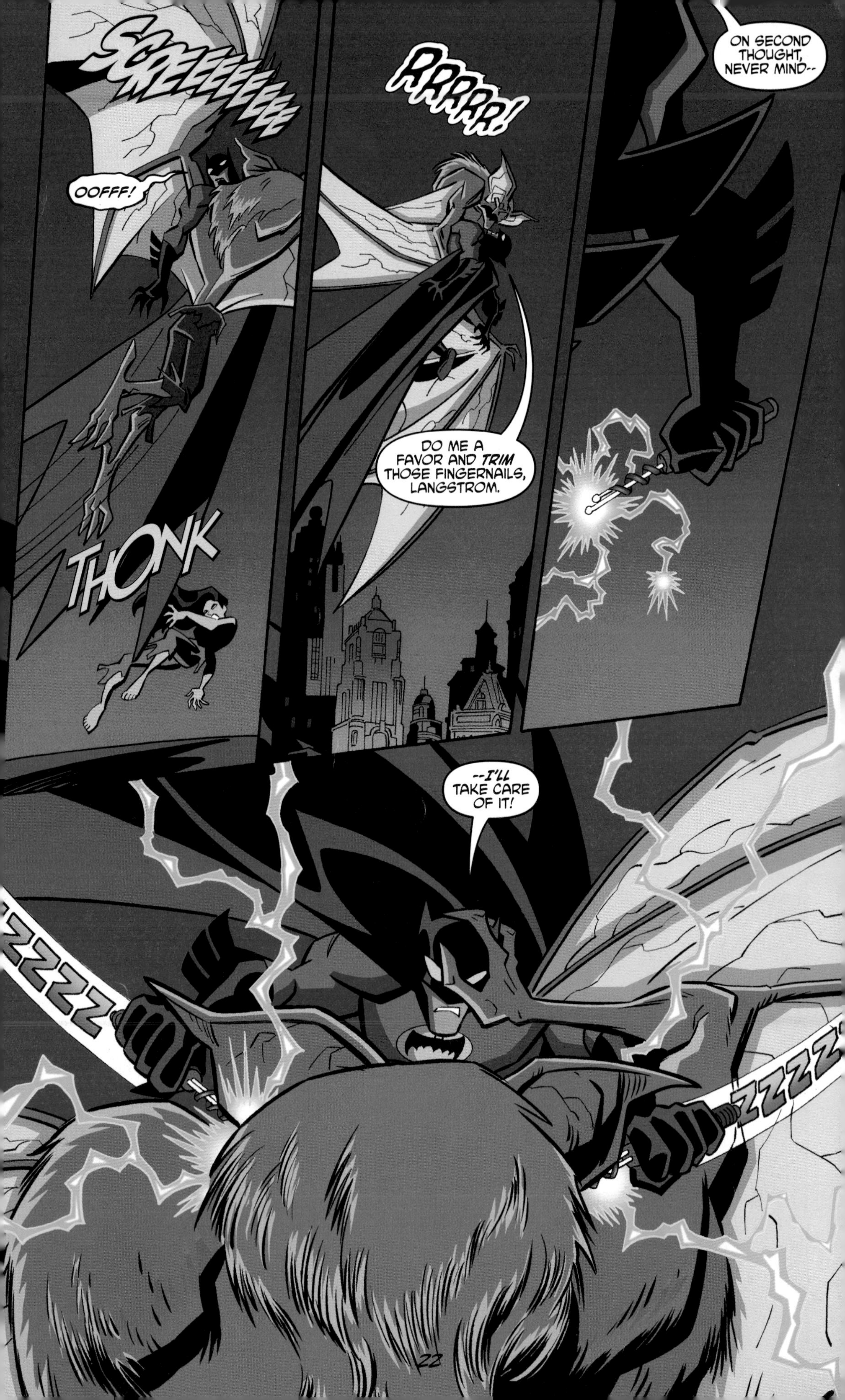
SCREEEEEEEEE
OOFFF!
THONK
RRRRR!
DO ME A FAVOR AND *TRIM* THOSE FINGERNAILS, LANGSTROM.
ON SECOND THOUGHT, NEVER MIND--
--*I'LL* TAKE CARE OF IT!
ZZZZZ
ZZZZZ

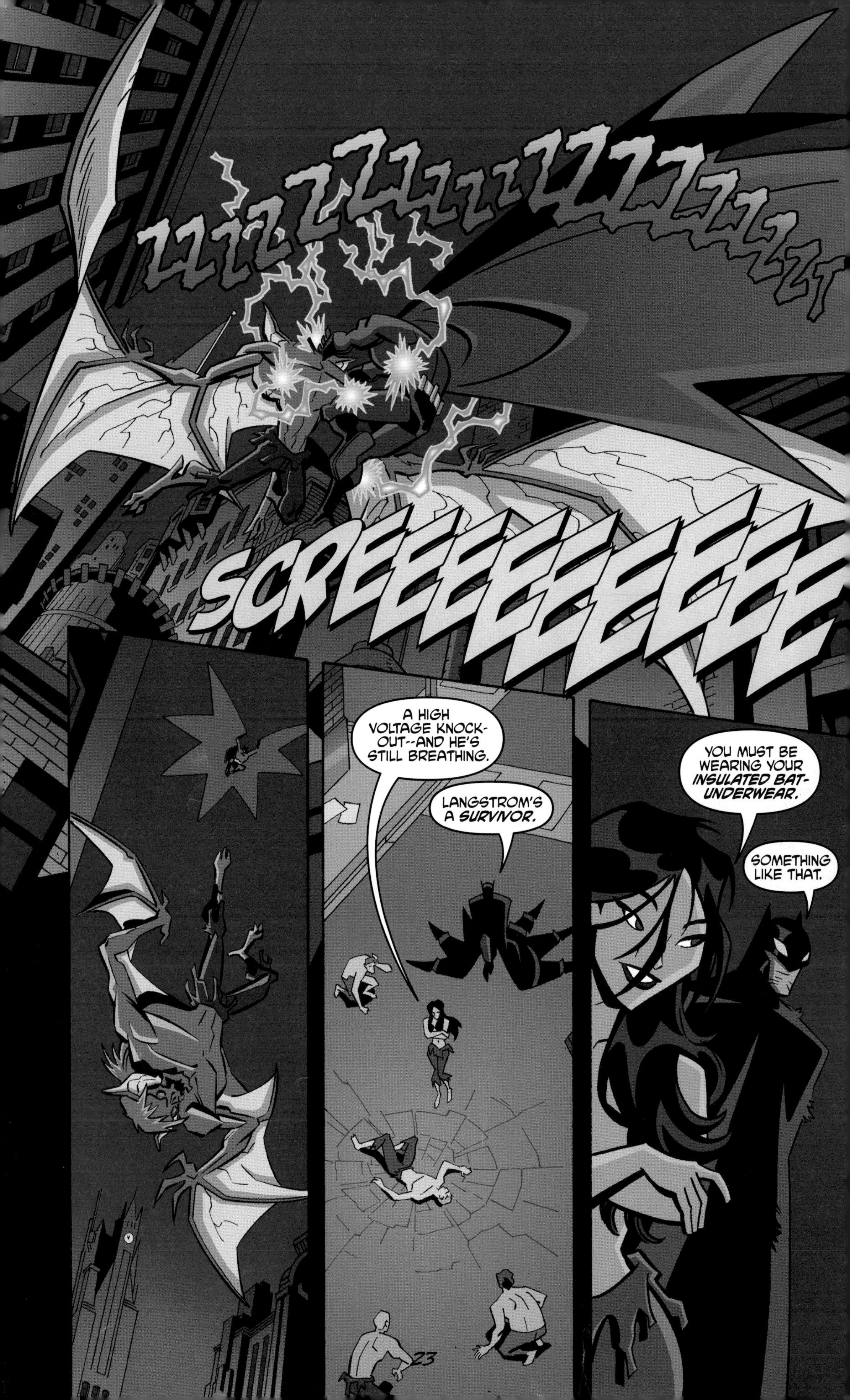
ZZZZZZZZZZZZZZZZZZZZZZZZZZT
SCREEEEEEEEEE
A HIGH VOLTAGE KNOCK-OUT--AND HE'S STILL BREATHING.
LANGSTROM'S A *SURVIVOR.*
YOU MUST BE WEARING YOUR *INSULATED BAT-UNDERWEAR.*
SOMETHING LIKE THAT.

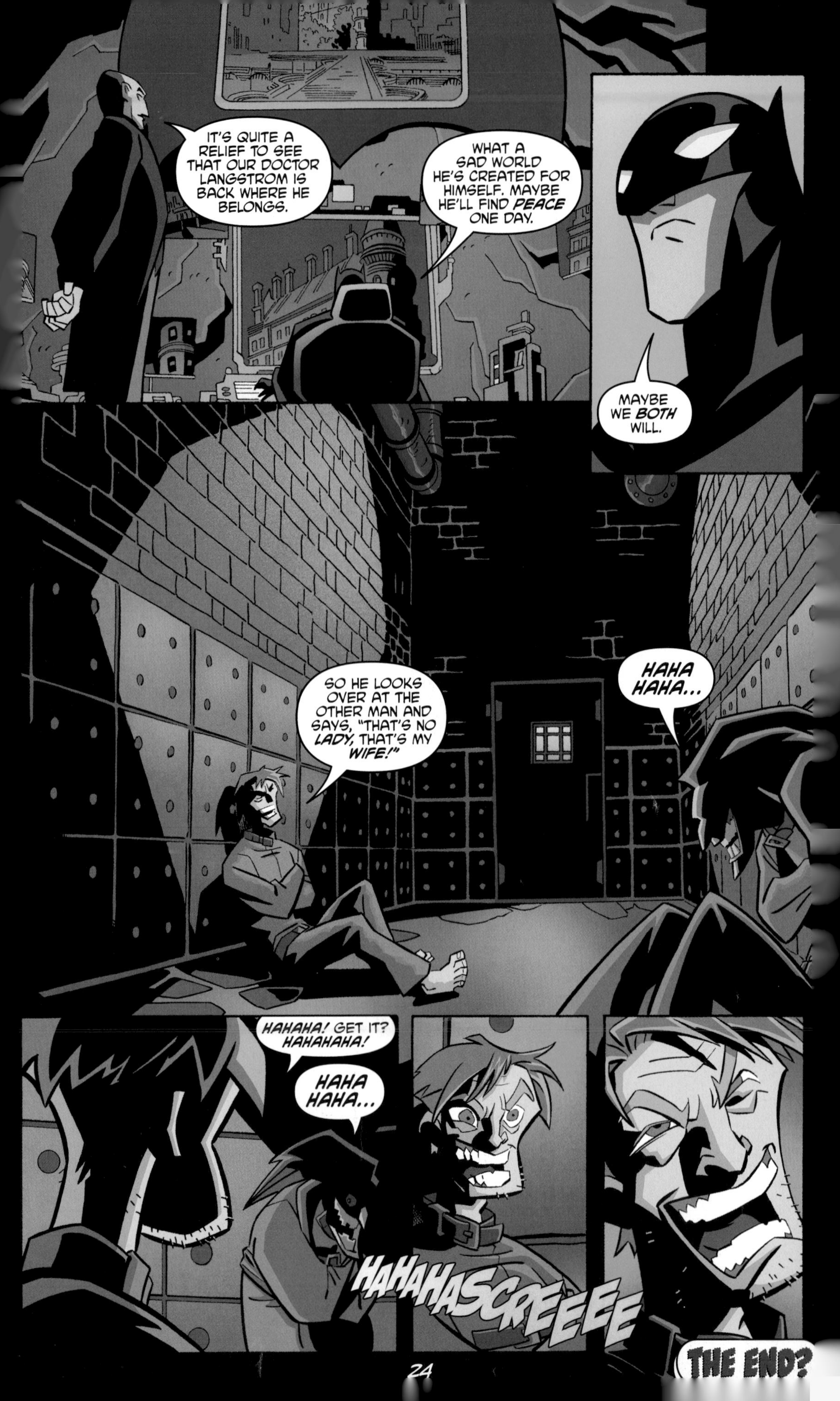
IT'S QUITE A RELIEF TO SEE THAT OUR DOCTOR LANGSTROM IS BACK WHERE HE BELONGS.
WHAT A SAD WORLD HE'S CREATED FOR HIMSELF. MAYBE HE'LL FIND PEACE ONE DAY.
MAYBE WE BOTH WILL.
SO HE LOOKS OVER AT THE OTHER MAN AND SAYS, "THAT'S NO LADY, THAT'S MY WIFE!"
HAHA HAHA...
HAHAHA! GET IT? HAHAHAHA!
HAHA HAHA...
HAHAHASCREEEEE
THE END?

CREATORS

BILL MATHENY WRITER

Along with comics like THE BATMAN STRIKES, Bill Matheny has written for TV series including KRYPTO THE SUPERDOG, WHERE'S WALDO, A PUP NAMED SCOOBY-DOO, and many others.

CHRISTOPHER JONES PENCILLER

Christopher Jones is an artist that has worked for DC Comics, Image, Malibu, Caliber, and Sundragon Comics.

TERRY BEATTY INKER

Terry Beatty has inked THE BATMAN STRIKES! and BATMAN: THE BRAVE AND THE BOLD as well as several other DC Comics graphic novels.

GLOSSARY

catastrophic (kat-uh-STROF-ik)--disastrous and destructive

formula (FOR-myuh-luh)--a rule or recipe in science or math that is written with numbers and symbols

insulated (IN-suh-lay-tid)--covered with material that stops heat or electricity from entering or escaping

mutation (myoo-TAY-shuhn)--genetic change

nosy (NOH-zee)--someone who is nosy is too interested in things that do not concern them

pathetic (puh-THET-ik)--feeble or useless

primitive (PRIM-uh-tiv)--very simple, uncivilized, or having to do with an early stage of development

rabies (RAY-beez)--a virus that attacks the brain and spinal cord and is spread by the bite of an infected animal

relief (ri-LEEF)--a feeling of freedom from discomfort, or help given to people in need

vial (VYE-uhl)--a small glass container used for holding liquids

vigilantes (vij-uh-LAN-teez)--individuals who take the law into their own hands

voltage (VOHL-tij)--the force of an electrical current as expressed in volts

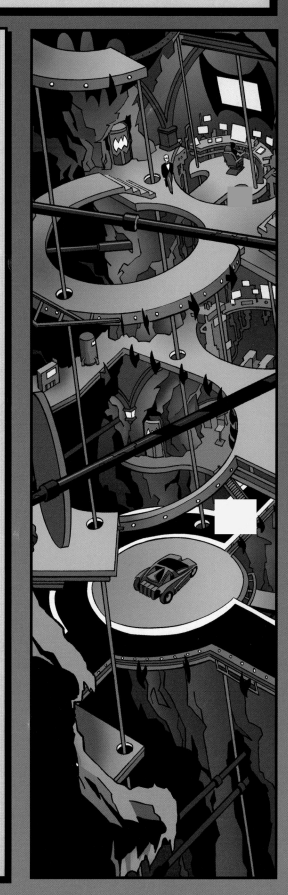

VISUAL QUESTIONS & PROMPTS

1. What do the circular lines around Batman's fist mean? [Hint: they are related to the sound effect at the top of the panel.]

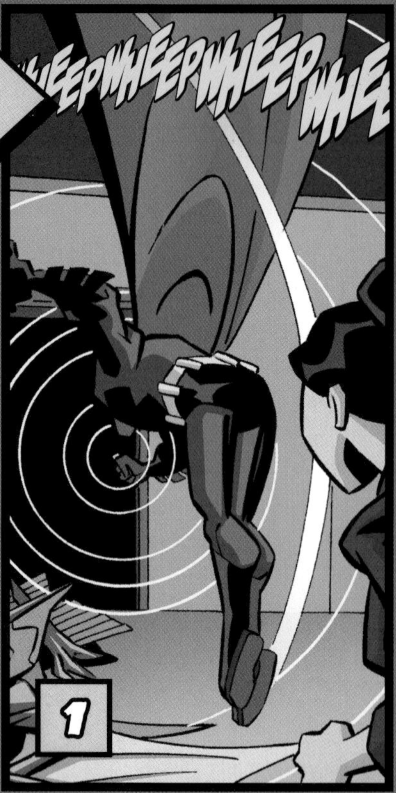

WHEEPWHEEPWHEEPWHEE
1

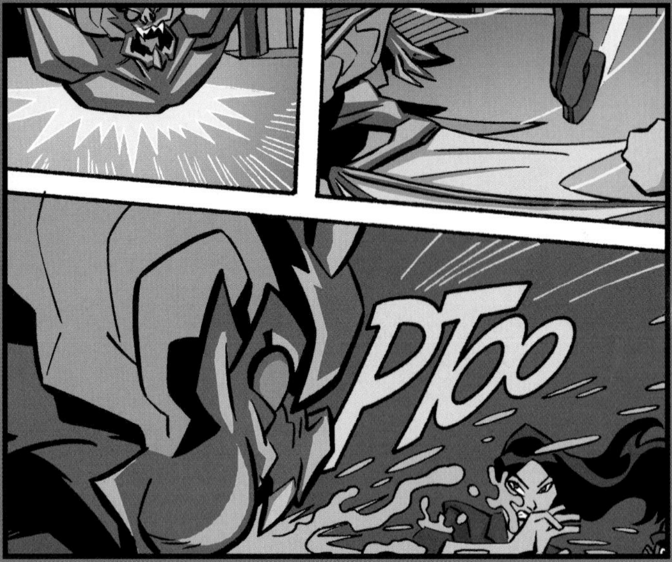

PTOO

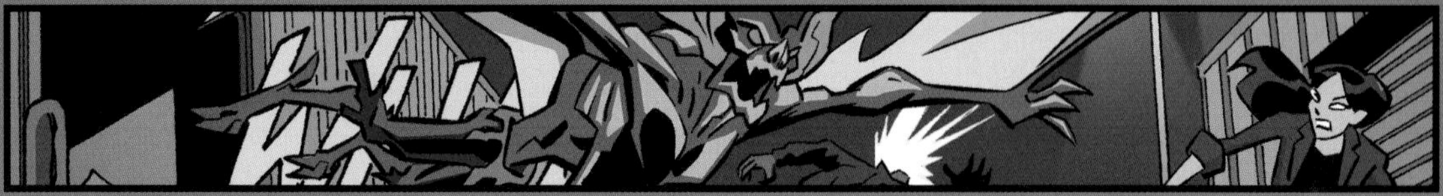

2. Why is the text in the two speech bubbles in the left panel smaller than the normal ones?

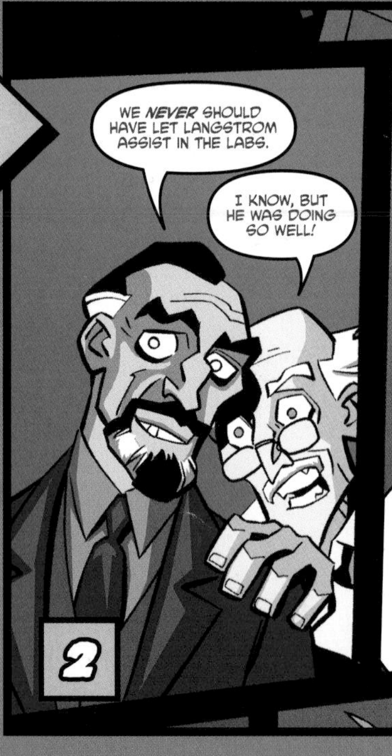

WE *NEVER* SHOULD HAVE LET LANGSTROM ASSIST IN THE LABS.
I KNOW, BUT HE WAS DOING SO WELL!
2

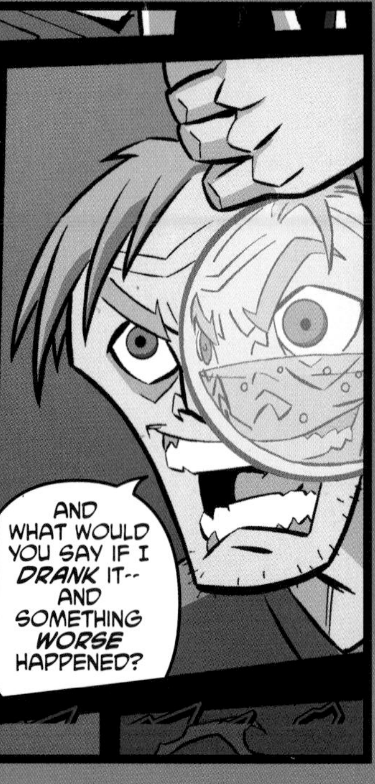

AND WHAT WOULD YOU SAY IF I *DRANK* IT-- AND SOMETHING *WORSE* HAPPENED?

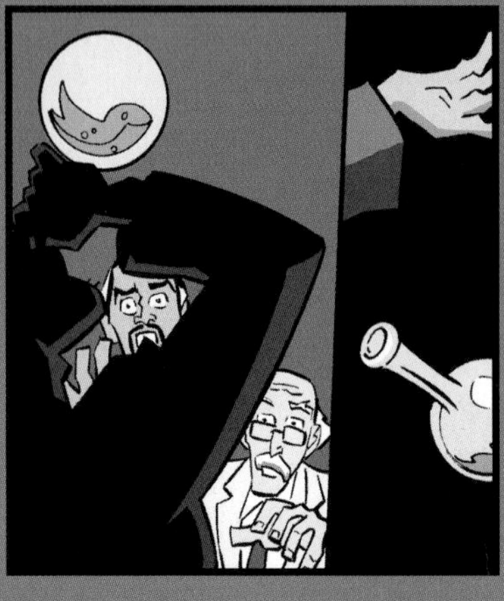

3. Batman's Utility Belt is filled with useful gadgets. Make a list of some other items that Batman might keep inside, and explain how they'd help him fight crime.

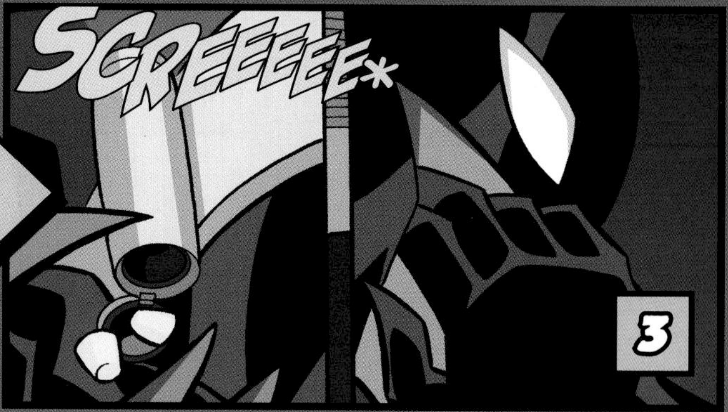
SCREEEEEE*
3

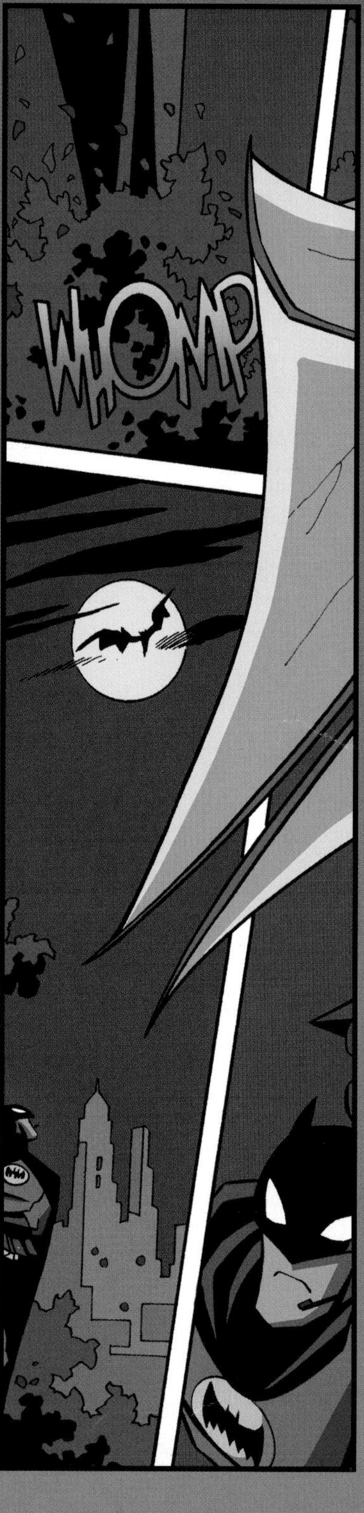
WHOMP

4. In the panel at the top right, we see the Man Bat's wings overlapping the panel borders. Why do you think the artists did this? How does the effect make you feel when you read this spread?

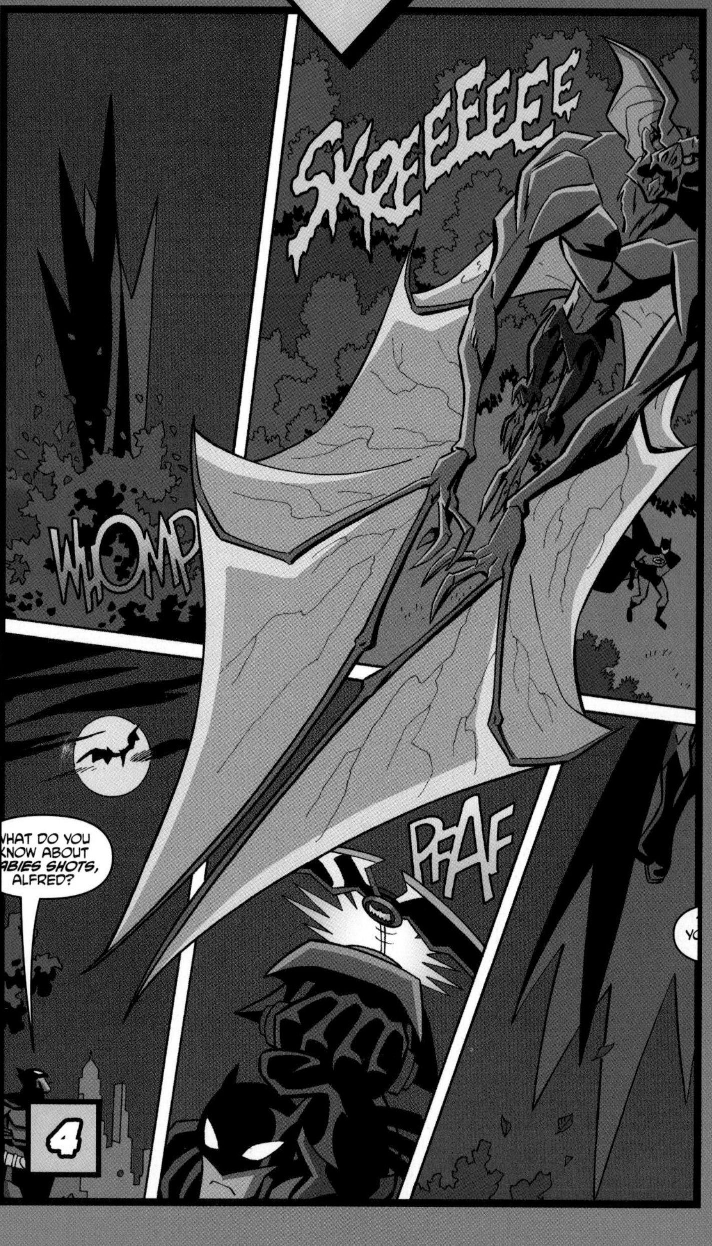
WHOMP
HAT DO YOU
NOW ABOUT
ABIES SHOTS,
ALFRED?
PFAF
4

READ THEM ALL!

THE BATMAN STRIKES!

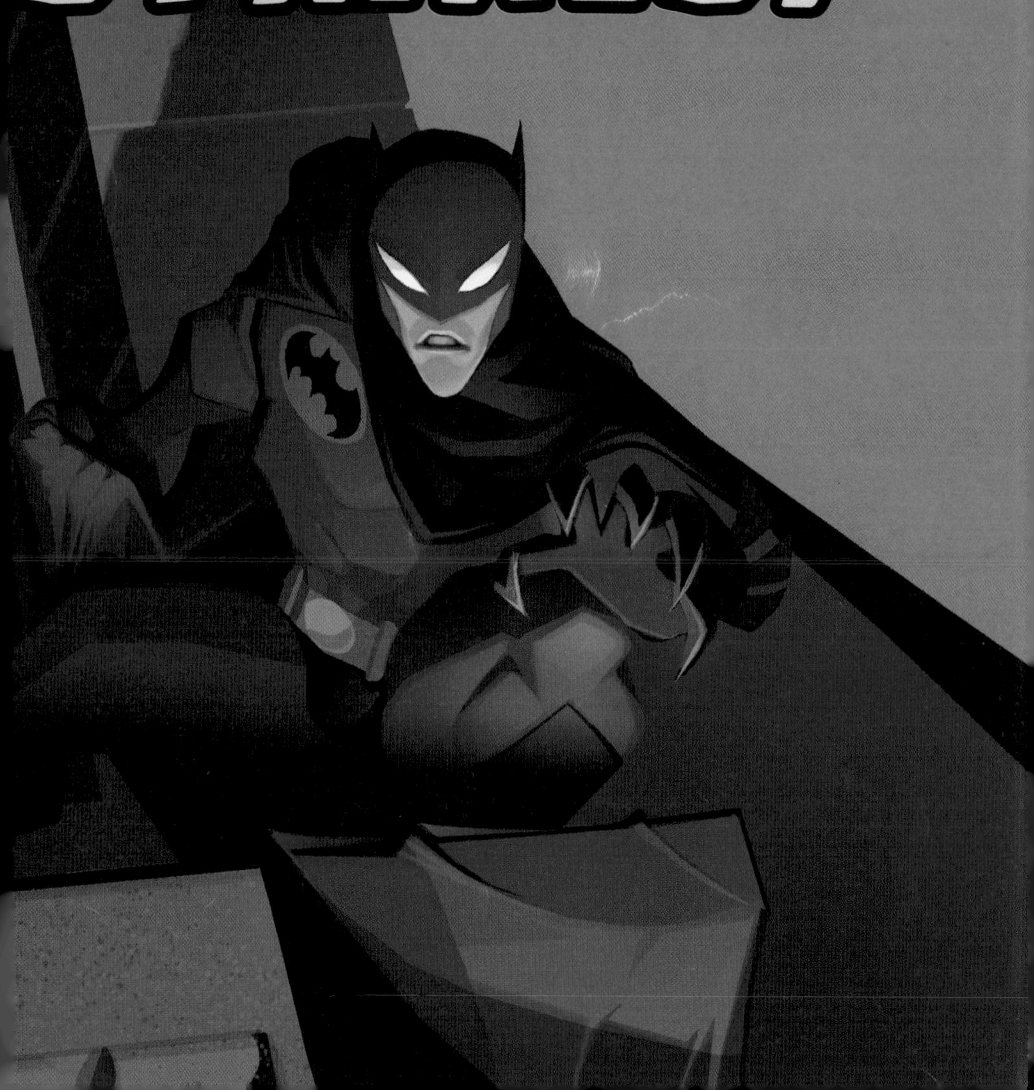

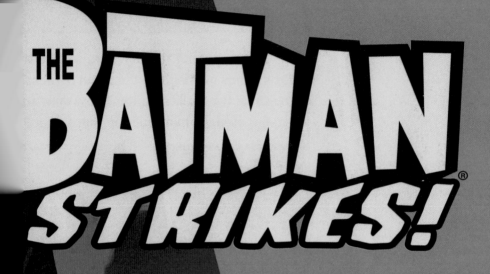

DC COMICS
THE BATMAN STRIKES!
IN THE CLUTCHES OF THE PENGUIN!
MATHENY · JONES · BEATTY

DC COMICS
THE BATMAN STRIKES!
BANE ON THE RAMPAGE!
MATHENY · JONES · BEATTY

DC COMICS
THE BATMAN STRIKES!
GOING... BATTY!
MATHENY · JONES · BEATTY

DC COMICS
THE BATMAN STRIKES!
Joker's Wild!
MATHENY
JONES
BEATTY

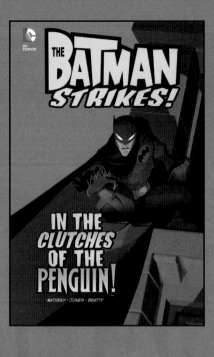

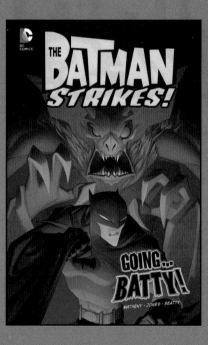